CHRISTOPHER PROIA

IF THEY KNEW
WHO HE WAS

BALBOA.
PRESS

A DIVISION OF HAY HOUSE

Balboa Press books may be ordered through
booksellers or by contacting:

Balboa Press
A Division of Hay House
1663 Liberty Drive
Bloomington, IN 47403
www.balboapress.com
1 (877) 407-4847

Print information available on the last page.

ISBN: 978-1-5043-9926-5 (sc)
ISBN: 978-1-5043-9927-2 (e)

Balboa Press rev. date: 03/13/2018

A NOTE FROM THE AUTHOR

Before reading, I must acknowledge some aspects of this story. The story is set during our own time period, and is based off the fact the President of the United States of America, becomes dictatorial, and creates chaos to his own people, and to the world. The story crosses many boundaries, multiple countries in the world are used, and a major political leader from another country is taken hostage. There is also a racial slur towards Hispanics that is said in the dialogue, but I mean no disrespect to any groups of people, due to the fact that it is a completely fictional story. This story is a worst-case scenario for the United States of America and I truthfully hope that we never live to see this world. I hope that with this story, some sort of peace can be obtained, or a lesson can be learned. This story may cause uneasiness towards the reader, but I have no intentions to demean anyone's culture, or ethnicity. I believe that as a world, if we, as the dominant world powers, work together, we can establish a glorified world, whose boundaries are unparalleled, and whose power will be unmatched. I hope that with this story, we can reach new heights that by ourselves would almost seem unattainable.

CHAPTER

The people were behind him; time after time he would win debates, and make promises that seemed attainable. In the limelight he was the best candidate, he would say what people wanted to hear, he would do what people wanted to see, and he would touch the humans spirit like no others have before. At his rallies, he would preach about transformation, and revamping society to reach a new peak. He believed that the Country he was conceived in had become weak, but with strong leadership he could make a change, for the better of his home. The people who gave him their ballets trusted his views, and accepted that a man with his stature should be the one to lead them. In all, he was thought as the answer to the people's prayers, and together they could make America great again.

Over time the man who was viewed as the best possible candidate finally won. In fact, he won by a landslide, and the Country collectively believed that something right finally happened, and by following him, they would be led towards virtue. At his final speech before accepting his presidency he vowed that choosing him to lead was the best option for society, and he would do anything in his power to succeed, even start wars.

His first decree was to forcefully remove all Mexican citizens out of his country, because he believed they were the source of the problems that he had to change. He believed that they were lazy people, and taking the jobs from all the people who now suffer from poverty in his home. To him, he saw all Mexican citizens as illegals, who jumped the border, so if he evacuated all of them, then the problem would be solved. His bill of the Extreme Discharge of Mexican Descendants was then proposed to congress, which was approved by the House of Representatives, and then approved by the senate. The bill would create evacuation sites where Mexican blooded citizens were supposed to gather, so they can be removed from society. Government officials were stationed at these evacuation sites, and they were sent house to house, for citizenship tests, to verify proper paperwork of an American citizen. If the person accused of being Mexican denied the removal from his or her home, for reasons of their own, then extreme actions were taken, from assaulting the person, destroying the person's home and property, or in the most extreme cases, death. This bill was passed and was about to become a law; so many people felt discomfort from it because of how barbaric it was. The next day, calamity broke out, but not only by Mexican citizens. Hispanics from every background stood side-by-side with their Mexican brothers and sisters in protest, because of how prejudice the governments views of these people were. The people were prepared for some sort of unjust views and laws from the soon to be dictatorial government, but they never thought the government would completely take the entire Mexican population out of the country, regardless of citizenship, so they would create a base camp where they would meet to talk about what their mission really was; a large number of Hispanics were living in Florida, so they would create an area there to conjugate, and discuss the future of the Hispanic population in America.

Over the next few days the Hispanics who occupied Florida began to get mail from the government, warning them if they did not cooperate with the law, then they would face serious consequences. The letters never said exactly what the punishment would be, but the people felt that no matter what it was it could not be good, so everyone crowded together to talk about the situation with the government, and to find a solution to the problem.

In the crowd, all people shared their views to decide how they would approach the government and who would lead them. After talking for hours a leader was finally decided, his name was Luis. Luis became the voice of the Hispanics because when he spoke others listened, he showed strength in a community that was suffering, and the others believed in him. He did not vote in the election, along with many of his Hispanic brothers, but when the bill was proposed and approved, he was prepared to step up as a leader for the Hispanic population. With his leadership the Hispanics became determined and comfortable in their roles, so on the next day, they would start their march to Washington.

While marching, the Hispanics were met at the border of Washington D.C. by armed government soldiers in bulletproof armor, and riot gear. Luis walked out to meet the cops to ask what the blockade was about. After two steps, a gunshot was fired, and struck the spot just in front of Luis's foot, causing the gravel to crush, and rocks to hop.

The head of the government's squad says, "If you don't turn around and go back to where you came from peacefully, we will open fire without restraint."

Luis responds, "We are here to protest this bill, and to try and get it appealed, we don't want a gunfight."

The man then says, "Well y'all know that y'all are rebelling against the government, so we have the right to shoot if necessary, but we would rather y'all be deported peacefully instead of facing death."

Luis says, "We are not turning around, or allowing one another to be deported, we are standing our ground until we can speak our peace."

The man then scolds Luis for his response. They continue to talk, and all the people do not appear to want a gunfight, but it is evident that the men will gladly shoot if they feel they need too.

What the government does not know though was that the Hispanics actually were prepared for a gunfight. Almost every person in the group had a weapon of some sort, some had handguns, multiple had machine guns, shotguns were around, and if you did not have a gun, you had a knife, bat, or other foreign object.

Another person in the group of Hispanics was named Tomás. While Luis was talking to the government trying to work out a solution, Tomás was devising a strategy in case a fight broke out between the two groups that would take out the government, and allow the Hispanics to be victorious. Him and others in the back of the group began to make Molotov cocktails to throw at the police, which would explode on impact causing flames and mayhem. The plan was to have the members with shotguns close to the front, so they could reach their targets, and to have the machine gunners behind the guys with shotguns. The men who only had melee weapons were scattered throughout the crowd ready to get low and bum rush the cops if shooting broke out. In the back

5

the people who had the Molotov cocktails were stationed, and if Luis gave the signal they were to throw the cocktails first to initiate the fight, hopefully blinding the enemies allowing better coverage for their own men.

Alcohol was filled in bottle after bottle, and rags were being soaked, but nothing was lit yet. Everyone was tense because even though the government thought it was a peaceful protest, they were still ready to shoot, and everyone knew one wrong move could get everyone killed. While Luis is still talking, one of the men within the Hispanics group lights a cocktail. In an instant, a shot was fired that hit the man who lit the cocktail in the heart, propelling his body a meter, and a loud thud was heard when his body hit the ground. A pool of blood slowly began to surround the body.

Then an officer shouted, "Fire!"

Guns started firing and slowly but surely bodies started to fall. Luis tried to yell something, but was quickly implanted with bullets. Four of them entered his body starting from the sternum, and then went down his body in a lightning bolt shape towards his gut. He fell, and the morale of the group of Latinos quickly joined.

Another person finally stepped up named Bruno, who was a big fellow.

He shouted, "Come on! Don't give up! We came to far to die without taking a few of them with us!"

Tomás rallied with Bruno and shouted, "Everyone fire!"

Then the Molotov cocktails were lit, and thrown at the government pigs. Once the blazing light of the cocktails began to illuminate the battlegrounds, everyone started rallying together. Morale slowly rose, and many people were not scared anymore, they knew on this journey they had already accepted their fate, and they knew no one can escape death, and if it is your time, then it is your time, they also knew that the people they were with right now were their brothers for life, and in the after life they would be taking tequila shots together for eternity.

The men with melee weapons rushed the enemies, remembering to stay low, because the bullets from the machine guns were fierce. Some died in the rush, but they did reach the enemy, one of the Hispanics took the knife he had, and stabbed an officer in the neck, pulling the blade out wildly, allowing a stream of blood to flow on soldiers on both sides. The line of officers in riot gear stood their ground though, and would deliver deathblows with handguns, or batons.

However, a ways down the line, Bruno had breached their defenses and was causing chaos for the enemy soldiers. Bruno charged the men in riot gear with three fellow Hispanic American soldiers, and with his squad they forced an opening in the line. The first man that Bruno attacked received a swift blow from a baseball bat to the skull, leaving an indent in the helmet of the officer. Bruno's partners followed behind the big man, and found openings behind the riot gear to attack. They would slash, bash, or impale any man in riot gear, for the death of their friends.

One of the men alongside Bruno named Diego noticed he was standing side-by-side with an officer, so he took his machete and proceeded to stab the man under his right armpit, which was the arm holding the riot shield. Diego kept the pressure until his blade was inside the man, and the man fell to the ground. Once on the ground Diego finally removed the blade that was covered in blood, but other men witnessed what he had done, and wanted to avenge their fellow comrade.

The commander of a patrol of men sent soldiers to reinforce the damage created by Bruno, but when the officers confronted the hole, they witnessed Diego slaying one of their own, so the men charged at Diego while he was starring at the dead man, frozen in fear, having never killed a man.

Diego was unaware of his surroundings or the situation he was in, and one of the officers who were charging at Diego finally reached him. The officer took his baton and smacked Diego's knee causing him to collapse. When Diego saw what was happening he counted that five men all equipped with weapons were surrounding him, but instead of executing Diego on sight, the men decided to jump him, they did not even use the weapons they had, but instead the first man kicked Diego in the face, and the others followed in the stomping.

Bruno saw Diego slowly dying with his own eyes, which infuriated him. He ran to help Diego, but was cut off by the rest of the squad of men immediately.

One man said, "Time to die big boy."

After the man says this Bruno charges at him, with bat in hand, and death on his mind. The man who said this then pulls out a pistol and shoots Bruno in the knee, immobilizing him. While on the ground the man walks to Bruno and stares at him as Bruno grips his knee tightly. The man then shoots Bruno another four times in his other leg, and in his stomach. Bruno was on his last breath when he saw the pistol rise again, but this time more slowly.

The soldier aims the pistol between Bruno's eyes, the last thing Bruno sees is the flash of the muzzle, and the last thing he hears is the loud bang from the gun.

After the trigger is pulled the Commander says to his soldiers, "Clean this spics mess up, we aren't gonna have his kind cleaning up for us anymore. Better to have them dead then illegal."

After Bruno is killed, the American government feels they have no more worries because in their eyes victory is certain. They fill the hole Bruno had created, and they killed the rest of the men who accompanied Bruno on his mission. The government soldiers mercilessly stomped out Diego until he became deformed and unidentifiable. Killing him in the end with their steel toed combat boots.

As for the other Hispanics, who were still fighting, they all would meet certain death.

When they formed a group rejecting the Presidents decree, and stationed it in Florida, they were already preparing for the worse. Once they marched to Washington, they crossed paths with the government at Washington's borders, and the government soldiers treated the Hispanics who marched as rebels. The pride that the Hispanics had was unmatched, and once conflict was initiated no one went back on their word. They kept fighting until the last man had fallen.

The final straw was when a Hispanic man accidently lit a Molotov cocktail creating panic, and much bloodshed for the Hispanic protestors.

CHAPTER

Time passed and many people were still shaken about the events that happened under the first decree of the president. Time may heal wounds, but no one could forget what really went down on that dreadful day. People were vigilant when they would see government officials, and they really did not know what was next. They felt that at any moment, war could break out, someone could be arrested, or even killed without reasonable cause. It was a time of fear, for the people under the new regime.

Over the next couple of months, secret organizations were beginning to form by the people. Some believed that the government under the new president was tyrannical and was a threat to the life of the common man and women. Through word of mouth, people began telling others about the groups that would try and rebel against the government. However, what the people did not know was that the President expected as much, and had already administered a secret police force that would pretend to be citizens, and would find information about the people who renounced the government. This was his second law, but no one knew he ever made it.

This law was forcefully passed in congress after a power struggle between the executive and legislative branches. Once the president obtained power he staged an assault on congress with his most trusted soldiers, they took their weapons and marched towards the United States Capitol building in D.C., where congress was stationed. Through all the calamity, and because the person who instructed the takeover was our Commander in Chief, the local police force did not know whether to side with the President or Congress, so they sided with the chief.

The police worked with the Presidents soldiers, went into the Capitol building and started destroying everything they could; art work, books, expensive decor, everything was vandalized that showed any weakness towards the new regime. The members of Congress who were inside the building tried escaping, but the soldiers and police were too much to handle, they pointed their guns at the members of Congress and made a hostage like situation. They allowed few to leave; only the people who believed in the President, and who swore their loyalty to him were freed. All who did not believe in the President would succumb to the madness that he always held. Once the members of Congress who sided with the President were released they went outside.

One member said to a soldier, "What's going to happen to the others who are still inside?"

The soldier replied, "Nothing good."

After that statement, a call was received on a Walkie Talkie.

It said, "Alright, theirs no one else in here who wants to be apart of our new society, should we carry out the execution orders?"

The soldier who stood next to the congressman then answered," roger that."

The next thing that was heard were gunshots from inside the Capitol building, screams were heard, everyone became distraught, and people began losing their hope for a brighter future. The wailing sounds, created chills down the spines of the ones who just barely missed death. They knew they were blessed for living, but they felt completely broken and betrayed, by who they thought would be the best possible leader, for the people.

After the building was ransacked, it was then set aflame because the documents inside could be used against the government. If normal people had access to these documents, then they could use this knowledge, and speak out against the government, and possibly create rebellions, which the President did not want.

In order to compensate for potential uprisings, he created a new law, which was in effect immediately after he stated it, due to the fact that he demolished congress, his law stated that the President was allowed to administer a police force in secrecy, so he could have complete control of the citizens, and no one could plot against the government.

The thing about this secret police force was that they were actually normal citizens who were promised fortunes beyond their wildest dreams. They were the people who never had anything, and when the opportunity came that if they snitched on their fellow man, and then they would be rewarded treasures in bulk, they took it. As for the people who were given the chance to be rats, but refused, they were put to death because the President and Government felt that they could not have any loose ends.

People began to talk, and word was spreading amongst the civilians like wildfire, but inside the civilian population were the Government's spies. One of the spies named Ian infiltrated one of the groups of rebellion, and became very close with the leader. He would always speak about how the government was corrupt, and that it needed to be overthrown. He began to have an influential presence towards the other members. Overtime, he became one of the major figures in the organization, whose word was respected amongst the rebels, giving him credibility throughout the commoner. In actuality, this man was a snake or a double crosser, he was promised wealth, safety, and a good life. Finally, after weeks of being an undercover, double agent, Ian compiled enough evidence to help the government devise a plan to take out the "terrorist group."

The trap was set for an assault on the organization that plotted against the Government. The one that Ian had attained credibility in, and had became one of the voices of, in the rebellion.

On this night, when the rebel group met to have one of their undisclosed meetings, meetings to create safety for the people, and to give them hope in a time of crisis, they would be met by malicious force, due to the spy who infiltrated their ranks.

Once everyone arrived and took their seats, they started to talk about how they would overthrow the Government, the leader of the group named Carl, noticed something different about the group who were present. Everyone was there except for one, Ian, when he came to this realization the doors abruptly opened, and men in armor came barging in, with no sense of restraint for the people inside.

The first men immediately ran straight to the stage where Carl was located, and with an automatic machine gun in hand he began to beat him with the stock of the gun until blood covered the stage he was on. While he was being attacked, the crowd was in awe, and more soldiers were taking over the area, pointing their guns at the men inside, and when one man tried to charge the armored official, he was quickly met with a bullet between the eyes.

This bullet caused a chain reaction inside the place, and then after, officers kept letting off bullets with intent to kill. The mission was never to take anyone hostage, or to imprison anyone, the mission was to eliminate the faction by any means.

While everyone was being taken care of by the officers, someone came into the place, solely, walking down the middle aisle towards the stage. He kept walking forward until he reached the stage and climbed onto it. The man walked up to the two officers who were beating Carl to death, and told them to stop. When Carl opened his eyes that were now bruised, misshapen, and too hard to fully see out of. He caught a glimpse of the man who told the other men to stop. It was his friend Ian, who he trusted from day one, one of the men that he thought would help him in his conquest to save America.

Carl says, "Ian?"

Ian does not reply.

Carl then whispers, "Do what you must."

With this last breath, Ian raises the gun that he was given by the Government soldiers, and pulls the trigger, completely forgetting about the past that they all had together, and how their purpose was to stop the Government.

After this scene, the two soldiers who were near Ian at the time began to console him, but Ian was not having it.

Ian then says, "I only did this because I wanted my family to survive, they were taken hostage and were put into a holding cell for the time being, I don't care if you think I did good or not, I just want the money I was promised."

With this statement, the soldiers looked at each other and knodded, they already new the real plan.

One soldier said to Ian, "You really think we were gonna give you money?"

Ian turns around in astonishment, and at this moment, a pistol was already drawn from its holster, and raised. The muzzle was pointed at his heart, and Ian's eyes grew large, he never thought that he would be double-crossed.

Then, with the pull of a finger, a bullet pierced his skin, causing his body to drop on the stage that he was on. He was still breathing, and the soldiers then closed the distance between them and him.

One soldier said to the other, "Well, this is another problem solved."

The other soldier says, "Yea, now we can go home."

With these statements, the soldiers raised their guns and shot him one final time in the forehead and walked away, leaving a pool of blood on the stage that Ian was now on, and they left all the other bodies in the room for the medical teams to clean up.

CHAPTER

After, once all the Mexican citizens had been removed, the strongest rebel group had been found, infiltrated, and annihilated, and the black community was demoralized, the next phase of the Presidents plan was underway, and it starts in Japan.

All the chaos at hand in the USA created a blanket to the world, while everyone was paying attention to the public, and the problems that the people were facing, the USA's government was still moving in the shadows, and they were continuing to execute their takeover strategy in secrecy.

The world was watching, most Countries were trying to speak with the President about his ideas, and they wondered why he was doing such dastardly deeds to his people. He would tell the world not to worry, and he made sure that he still would have alliances with some Countries in the world. He made it clear that he was already friends with France, Great Britain, and Germany, and he swore that if anything happened to them, he would mobilize his U.S. American troops to help their cause.

He told his allies that war was a possibility, he met with the leaders of France, Great Britain, and Germany to talk plans, and how he would precede going forward. One thing he wanted to make happen was a peace treaty with Japan.

The President called the emperor of Japan and asked if they could have a meeting, regarding a peace treaty, or an alliance between the two Countries. The Emperor of Japan was hesitant in trusting the chief diplomat of the United States of America, but the Emperor agreed to the meeting regardless, the only stipulation was that the meeting needed to take place in Japan. The President obliged.

While on his flight to Japan, the President brought with him two trusted secret service agents to accompany him. They were only there to protect the President, not to be hostile towards the citizens, or any other government official. While on his decent, when he landed on the runway, and the plane stopped, he was greeted outside of the plane, by the Emperor of Japan, at Haneda airport.

The connection between the two leaders was immediate when they started to talk; they used translators, because the President of the USA had not fully grasped the language yet. The Emperor of Japan invited the President to the National Diet of Japan, and they started to negotiate peace between the nations, and they talked about making an alliance for the future. Their were no hostilities at their meeting, because the meeting was about making a friendship, but one other aspect of the talk was important, the fact that the President wanted to takeover China, and he wanted to work with the Japanese, to conquer the Country, by using any means necessary.

This was a secret talk between the United States and Japan, no other Country, nor their leaders knew of this scheme, and the President wanted to keep it that way. He knew that the other Countries would be against it, so he wanted to keep it just between the two nations.

Once the Japanese Emperor found this out, he was hesitant, but due to the long history between the Chinese and Japanese, he wanted revenge, and agreed with the Presidents decree to takeover China. The agreement was that the USA would send undercover agents into Japan, and these people would help militarily, by devising strategies with the smartest Japanese, for an assault on China. The reason why he needed Japans help was because they knew the landscape of China better than the United States. With their knowledge, the chances of success became greater.

Another clause in the agreement was that the plan would be completely "in the dark", meaning that no other Country knew what would be happening once the plan was settled and finalized.

After this talk, the President and his two agents left via jet, and already started planning their next step. Once they got home the President started sending soldiers and agents alike in plain clothes to Japan. Once the people got there, they were given credentials that allowed them access into the Japanese embassy, and credentials that allowed them on the streets. Overtime, slowly, more and more soldiers from the USA began to flood into Japan's streets and into their government. The thing was, there was a secret plan, which the American government devised. Once they executed their real plan, all American soldiers were to terminate as many Japanese officials, or possible threats as they could.

The Japanese trusted the United States so much; they even allowed two armed American special agents, the same ones that came with the President originally, to help stand guard for the Japanese Emperor.

While standing guard, in the office of the Emperor of Japan, the agents got an order through their earpiece.

The soldiers heard, "Time to execute plan Tsunami."

The soldiers responded, "Roger."

In that instance, the soldiers who were guarding the Emperor, drew their pistols, and began to shoot at everyone in the room.

They never thought twice because they knew exactly what they were sent there to do, and the Japanese were so caught off guard, they almost had no time to react.

They were the first to initiate the plan, and they were the ones who stood right next to the Emperor of Japan. They killed everyone in the room, but they left the Emperor alive as a hostage, but they would act as if he were dead, so the morale of the Country would take a major hit and the people would feel defeated.

After the killings inside the room, and taking the Emperor hostage, the order for plan Tsunami reached all other US American soldiers in the Country. No one was safe and people everywhere were scared for their lives.

However, the fight was not as easy as expected, for the US Americans, many of these soldiers would lose their lives, but the surprise attack gave them a true advantage.

On the streets of Tokyo, was where an onslaught took place, the US Americans with their fully automatic machine guns, let bullets fly, taking out anyone in their way, the Japanese police would fight back, but the power of the heavy weaponry the US Americans brought, and the surprise tactic, completely stunned the Japanese.

The US Americans were everywhere, dressed in plain clothes, and some had bulletproof vests. The hardest part for the Japanese, were that so many Americans had already infiltrated the Japanese National Diet, because of the "peace treaty", so wherever a Japanese person would go, there would already be US Americans ready to shoot. Nowhere was safe for the Japanese officials, or the Japanese citizens.

The final deciding factor was when the US Americans seized the armory inside the Parliament. Once they had control of this, they had total control, because if Japan did not have weapons, then they could not fight back.

The assault on the armory was were most US Americans lost their lives. To reach the weapons, the US Americans needed to move down a long corridor, but the Japanese were prepared for this, and they had it protected with their own powerful weapons.

Once they reached the corridor, a Japanese soldier shouted, "Fire!"

And a barrage of lead bullets followed, piercing the bodies of many US American soldiers, who entered the long hallway. Once the US Americans realized that the hallway was locked down, they did not proceed, so no other soldiers would be wounded, or die.

The captain of the squad says, "throw some flash and smoke grenades, we need this armory at all costs!"

After that statement the flash bang grenades were thrown, followed by smoke grenades, and the soldiers activated thermal optics to see through the smoke, so they could attack the Japanese and control the armory

The Japanese were blinded, and shocked that the Americans betrayed them; while the smoke was still dense they continued firing. The Americans could see the bodies of the Japanese through the smoke, by reading their heat signatures.

It was a suicide mission to get to the armory, but the Americans needed control of the weapons, so they charged when the captain gave the orders.

The captain says, "Follow me."

He turned the corner and sprinted into the smoke with his soldiers behind him, he could see the heat radiating off the enemy. He continued to shoot while running, but about halfway down the corridor he was hit in the leg, and collapsed. When his men saw this they tried to drag him out. The soldier who tried to help was also shot, but his wound was fatal, he was shot through the neck, as he bent over to try and help the captain.

When he was shot, the blood splattered across the captain's face, and the image scarred the captain, but he still did not want to give up.

The captain, who was now shaken, shouted, "Don't worry about me, focus on the mission at hand. We need this armory or we will never have complete control!"

With that statement a new fire was awakened in the soldiers, they started running and gunning, without worrying about their own lives. Bodies began falling on both sides, but a majority of the casualties came from the US Americans.

After much persistence, they finally reached the doorway and completely bum rushed the people through it, and ransacked all the supplies in the armory. The first Japanese soldier was met with the butt end of the gun, to the face, shattering his teeth. The second and third soldiers got lit up, with bullets to the chest.

After the blockade was broken, and the Americans busted into the armory, the Japanese became overwhelmed. The Americans outnumbered them two to one inside the armory, and were brutal, and malicious in their attempts to seize the weapons.

In a way the US Americans were barbaric, shooting at anyone who tried to stop them. After this bloody battle, the armory was seized by the US, but the casualties were excruciating for the US Americans.

They captured the Japanese embassy, and took control of the Country.

CHAPTER

While the world was trying to solve the problem with America, the Americans proceeded to initiate another phase to their plan. They decided to attack the Middle East, specifically Afghanistan.

They sent military soldiers, specifically a team to take out military soldiers in Afghanistan, so they could take the oil and the land of the Country.

They sent a squad of thirty men to a specific spot in the country, all armed with M16 machine guns. These soldiers were told that they needed to take out as many enemy soldiers as possible, or anybody that got in their way.

The assault of the Middle East was being televised in America as a kind of propaganda that was being pressed on the men, women and children of the new regime, and because of this the people of Afghanistan were prepared for an invasion. One plane carried a squad of thirty men. The American soldiers already stationed in the Country were controlling a specific area, so the plane could land on the soil. The way the American soldiers in the Country obtained the area was by a use of force to make the area free of Afghanistan citizens. Once the American soldiers freed open the area that allowed the American soldiers to land the plane, there was a panic in the Country because the Americans were on their land, and ready to kill for their cause.

Once landed, the soldiers of Afghanistan were prepared for a fight, and they surrounded the area that was being controlled by the hostile Americans. The Americans did not think much of the enemy soldiers because the Americans felt that they were more prepared and better trained, also they were still using AK-47's, and the guns of the Americans were much more advanced and accurate.

Once landed the Americans took control of a building, by using practiced moves and techniques to kill the enemy soldiers inside, and across the way, the Afghanistan soldiers controlled another building, the Afghans were stationed in different windows of the four-story building they were occupying, their were three windows on the top and two on the bottom, and the middle window on top of the building was larger so two people would be shown at a time, one on each side, and four people would be present at a time on the top, while two people would be shown at the bottom. Meanwhile the Americans were stationed behind the building they controlled across from the Afghanistan troops.

The building that the Americans were stationed in was originally controlled by enemy troops. The Americans were prepared for the building to be occupied, and attacked accordingly, killing the enemy was easy as clearing the landing zone for the plane was. The building the Americans were in was in the shape of an L. One side was a wall with a single door that the Americans came in to take the building. There was no roof and the other side was a wall with two window openings that faced the enemy soldiers. The building was completely destroyed, but it was an area where the Americans could get a clean look at the enemy and shoot their guns under some cover.

The Americans were standing in an opening behind the wall of the building on the ground, and only four soldiers would shoot, and be exposed at a time. Across the way the Afghans were stationed throughout the building in multiple windows on each story, exposing many men, and displaying to the Americans many targets. This made the Americans feel at even more of an advantage because they felt that since the Afghans were everywhere throughout the building, this displayed more targets to be shot by the Americans, and the artillery of the Americans were also A-class, and they were better trained because they had more battle experience, so the Americans did not shake or fret about what the outcome of this battle would be.

Between the two buildings was a giant space, and the wind was blowing ferociously. While the Afghan soldiers were using their AK-47's, and were shooting across this giant space, their bullets were scattered all over the place because of the air resistance. The Americans with their M16's were much more accurate, and this showed to be a major strength for the American soldiers.

They would shoot and the three round burst made the shots easier to judge, and they started to kill many Afghanistan soldiers, in the building. While all the American soldiers were clustered in the one opening, only sending in four soldiers at a time, they decided to send their best shooters around the building to get another angle on the enemy.

The captain says, "Chris, Joe, go around the building and target the enemy from another angle."

Chris who was the best shooter on the squad hesitated and said, "Are you sure we should go around, it might take our lives."

The captain then says, "You know what you signed up for, and you knew that death was a possibility. You have to go."

Chris says, "Alright, lets go Joe."

With that statement the two soldiers snuck around the left side of the building, getting another angle on the enemy.

Chris quietly says, "Let me shoot first, and don't fire until I give you the okay."

There was an opening and another wall on the left side, so Chris barrel rolled across the gap, and hid so the enemy did not see him. Once the two soldiers were stationed in their spots, Chris told Joe to hold.

Chris leaned around the corner and poked his gun out; he aimed at an enemy soldier on the top floor of the building across from them, and shot. He missed his first shot and took cover again; luckily the enemy did not notice him. He realized that his shot was off by about three meters because of the air resistance, so he leaned past the wall again, and this time when he shot he hit his target. He then moved onto his second target, shot, and killed him too. Then he hit the third, and fourth, but after the fourth target was shot, he was detected, and the Afghan soldiers started shooting at him.

When they started firing at him, He turned to Joe and yelled, "Start shooting I've been detected!"

Now both soldiers were firing and the Americans were also shooting from the original spot. Chris hit two more targets, and then all of the Afghan soldiers were taken out. The two shooters that came around the left side of the building returned to their squad.

Chris was shaken when he returned due to all the bloodshed that he caused, and once the captain confronted him, he pulled out his handgun on his fellow soldiers, and shakily began to point the pistol at them.

The captain said, "Relax your mission is done, you don't need to be vigilant anymore."

Chris was hesitant and almost instantly regretted what he had done, but the mission was complete, and he was able to return back to the squad.

The captain says, "you did good now rest, we will confirm the bodies of the people you shot, so just relax and head back to base."

The rest of the squad of men proceeded forward, and started taking more and more territory, after a while the group of men confronted another group of Afghan soldiers, and initiated in another gun fight.

The Afghan soldiers did not give up, and continued fighting for their lives and for their Country. Most of the soldiers who were fighting were everyday workingmen and husbands, they also had soldiers who were sixteen years old fighting on the front lines. Many people had been recruited, and the Middle Eastern people continued to feel the pressure from the Americans, but they did not want to give into the Capitalist regime because they were fighting for something else, something more precious to them, their home.

The people of the Country, who were now soldiers, wanted to make sure their families were safe, and they wanted their Country to be secure, and intact, but the pressure of America was excruciating and overwhelming.

The American soldiers continuously sent more troops to Afghanistan, so the pressure for the Afghans would be too great to handle, and after fighting for days they finally reached the capital, and once the capital was taken they knew the mission was complete.

The soldiers took the oil refineries in the Country, and won their war, which was completely unnecessary in the long run. They acquired the oil that they wanted, but the cost was great. Many American soldiers died, and many Afghan soldiers lives were also lost, but the Americans lost much more lives when a suicide bomber bombed one of the major groups of soldiers. After this conquest, the oil refinery was taken, and many soldiers died on both sides, but the goal of the Americans was accomplished.

Overtime, the soldier Chris was referred to as a hero, and he was given a promotion, the promotion was to join an elite squad of soldiers who would do the dirty work of the regime. They were high-class soldiers whose mission was to take out as many enemy combatants as possible. They would do top secret missions that the government personally distributed to them.

Chris began to complete all his missions with high proficiency, and eventually he too became a commander for his own squad of soldiers. He started on simpler tasks when he first became a commander, but eventually his success rate of each mission became great, and he started getting more hard missions to execute.

While Chris was home, he was just like any other man, he had a family, and he had a wife who was pregnant waiting for him after every mission, always worrying. She was his number one fan and the love they shared was strong and large.

Every time Chris left the house he would hear, "I love you."

And he always responded with, "I love you too."

They were just normal people living in times under the harsh regime, but they never though too much about it, they believed what was happening and what they did was for the better, so they lived their lives care free, except for when Chris would travel on his high class top secret missions.

Chris's wife was also a nurse at a hospital; the hospital she worked at was a major hospital for wounded soldiers. Many people would come thru and she always would help the best she could. Some were too wounded for treatment while others she had saved, and sometimes their were even small wounds, that would be treated, so she too had knowledge, and she had seen her fair amount of bloodshed during these times of war.

One day both Chris and his wife were at the house just watching T.V. together and talking.

Then suddenly the phone rang and the person on the other line was Chris's old commander, and he said "Chris we have a mission for you, I need you at this location at this time."

Chris said, "roger that."

Then Chris hung up the phone and started packing his things.

His wife asks," Where are you going this time?"

Chris said," An outpost on the border at Russia, Don't worry I'll be ok."

Chris's wife said, "Ok just be careful."

He says," Of course as always."

He then got together all his things, and he made one more check just to be sure.

He is about to leave and his wife says," I love you."

He replies, "I love you too."

And with that statement Chris leaves his home, ready for anything the world has in store for him.

A while later Chris arrives with his team to the designated location. They were all ready for battle, they had all their equipment, and their confidence was high.

They were taken to a location inside a base, and their mission was to protect the base while Russian soldiers infiltrated.

Chris's squad was of four soldiers including Chris, and they knew that the enemy soldiers also had a team of four invading the base.

The interior of the base was that there was a drop between the front and back of the base. On top of the drop there was multiple walls, there were two walls about a yard tall on the top of the drop, and another wall to the left of the walls. On the bottom portion of the drop there was multiple walls scattered throughout the bottom. Chris stationed two soldiers to the closest to the drop in a left and right location behind the walls, they were to wait until the enemy came in and were to shoot to kill them. Chris and another member of his squad were stationed in the back of the walls, to act as a secondary defense to the invading soldiers if the first two soldiers were to die.

It was silent in the base, and all the soldiers were stationed in their designated spots. All of a sudden two enemy soldiers ran out from behind the walls shooting and crouching, they were met with bullets from Chris's squad. They were engaged in the firefight and both sides were showcasing their skills, but Chris's soldiers died in the end. Then the two enemy soldiers proceeded forward.

The soldier who was with Chris says, "What should we do Chris?"

Chris replies, "Throw some flash bang grenades and be prepared to shoot the enemy."

They both threw their flash bang grenades and shot up behind the walls, but they were quickly met with two shots to both their heads, and the Russian soldiers killed Chris and his partner.

Back at home Chris's wife was worried because she had not seen her husband Chris is a long time, she keeps thinking that something bad might of happened.

One day she was at the hospital and a body came in, it was her husband Chris, and he was dead on the stretcher he came in on. His wife could not take it and dropped to her knees and started to cry over his dead body. The fellow medics around her began to console her, but they also needed her to gather her composure and do what she needed to do for work.

Chris was regarded as a hero to many, under the regime of the president, but he was killed in the line of duty while trying to protect his home.

CHAPTER

After the conquest, and the assault on Japan, the world was shocked and disappointed with America. They never thought their would be a double cross, and they thought that they could trust the US Americans, but it was evident that the USA were working on their own terms, without regards to the people who they made peace with.

The world decided that the actions the USA took were unjust, and discipline needed to take place. The first action the world took was to kick the USA out of the League of Nations. This was to show the USA that the whole world meant business, and would not tolerate the crimes committed by the USA. Then, the leaders of all other nations decided that they would attack the USA, so they gathered together at a disclosed location to devise a strategy.

What the world wanted to do was liberate Japan, and fight the USA on American soil. The problem was that Canada and Mexico bordered north and south of the USA, so they needed to have these Countries agree upon an alliance with the other Nations, who wanted to take out the United States of America. Mexico agreed to an alliance because of the law against the Mexican citizens, but Canada was hesitant, due to the fact that they have always been friends with the United States of America.

However, they also saw what the USA was becoming, which was a tyrannical government who would rule with an iron fist, so they understood that the USA was wrong. After contemplating these facts, Canada then agreed to the alliance against America.

All of the heavy hitting nations were part of the alliance, these nations included, Russia, Great Britain, France, Germany, Spain, Portugal, Australia, India, China, Canada, and Mexico.

The first part of the plan was to liberate Japan, so Germany and France sent troops, and artillery power to China; this is where the world would start their attack.

While this was happening, Great Britain and India would work together to hold down the Atlantic Ocean; patrolling and making sure the US American boats could not cross their blockade.

Meanwhile, Australia, Spain, and Portugal sent their land troops to Mexico in order to give the USA a fight at its southern border; they also had boats ready in the Gulf of Mexico. The Royal Navy also had boats in the Pacific Ocean.

The last piece was Russia, in agreement with Canada, they sent a massive number of land troops into Canada, they came through Alaska and went South East, so they were close to New England and the capitol of the United States of America.

With all the pieces set, the world was finally ready to wage a war with the USA. The first action that took place was to attack the US Americans in Japan, so all the soldiers in China began the assault with their air force, the Germans brought a navy, and U-boats to sink the USA's naval fleet, and France brought an army, navy and air force for the cause.

The battle for Japan was a battle between air forces and navies. The problem for America was it did not have enough manpower in Japan to fully fight them off. While fighting, many pilots would be killed, and many boats were sank, but persistence was key, and eventually, some boats made it to the coast of Japan, and now there were land forces in Japan ready to fight. The US Americans did not want to fight on land, due to the limited number of people, and the unfamiliarity of the landscape. They did not want more casualties, so they decided to retreat back to the USA under direct orders from the President.

On their voyage home, the royal navy intercepted them, this was a turning point in the war, the royal navy attacked the weakened US Americans, and this became the Battle of the Pacific. The Royal

Navy outnumbered and out maneuvered the US troops, and eventually, all the boats that tried to return home were destroyed.

The President started to panic because he never thought that all these nations would work together, and while he was panicking, he got word of an attack at the Mexican border, so he decides to send troops to the Mexican border, but he was still worried of an assault by Great Britain on the western coast, so he sent troops to California as well, in case of an invasion by Great Britain. What the President did not think about though, was that he was protecting two fronts, which was not a smart military tactic.

The battle at the Mexican border was gruesome; many men lost their lives on both sides. Machine gun fire sounded like crashes of lightning, and the dirt became red from the blood of fallen soldiers. The smell was death, and it was lingering in the air, wave after wave of soldiers kept rushing to their graves. The land became covered with bullet filled carcasses, but the soldiers knew that they needed to stop USA at any means.

While the Americans were fighting at the Mexican border, the Russians began their advance through New England, coming from Canada. The President was astonished that Canada made a treaty with Russia, and he decided to move himself and the other troops, towards the middle of the Country. Russian Forces were met by American soldiers. The numbers were completely in Russia's favor. The President miscalculated the situation, by putting his soldiers on three fronts of battle, because they were undersized in numbers on every front.

The President ordered his troops from overseas to come back to help, but on their way back they were met by another Great Britain fleet, this fleet also had power from India. Now, there was a battle at the Mexico border, on the Atlantic Ocean, and the Russians were progressing southwest from New England.

The USA was caught in a pickle, and was being attacked from all sides. All the other nations were squeezing USA into submission. The Royal Navy and The Royal Indian Navy fleets fought the US Americans on Atlantic water, and won, for the problem was America was divided, and did not have enough manpower in any battle. After a while the United States of America's President was surrounded, with limited soldiers, and many enemies.

Then, while the President was surrounded, a letter came from Great Britain, It said, "Surrender, or we will give Russia word, to proceed with the attack."

The President did not give in.

On the last day of the stakeout the Russian soldiers advanced, with their bullets they would kill

American soldier after soldier, until they reached the President.

Once face to face with the President, A Russian soldier said, "Life or Death?"

The President responds, "Death."

With that statement, a bullet was delivered between his eyes. And the reign of the best possible candidate was over.

THE END

ABOUT THE AUTHOR

Christopher Lawrence Proia is a newcomer to the writing scene, he is from Newton, Massachusetts, and is a carry out worker at a local Bertucci's restauraunt. He has worked many jobs, from being the dairyman at a supermarket, to being a camp counselor in the summertime. As a young kid he was a member of the John M. Barry Boys and Girls Club, and became youth of the year in 2014 after being a member of the club since he was five. He graduated from Newton North High school; then pursued a degree from the University of Hartford, but later transferred after a couple years, to attend Massbay Community College due to an incident that happened at his school. He has never left the United States or has been on a commercial airline but he is eager to travel, and experience new sights, and journeys.

He became interested in politics after the previous election, and he wrote his book based on a worse case scenario for the world in response to the election.